THE FARM THAT RAN OUT OF NAMES

THE FARM THAT RAN OUT OF NAMES

William Mayne

JONATHAN CAPE
LONDON

First published 1990
© William Mayne 1990
Jonathan Cape Ltd, 20 Vauxhall Bridge Road,
London SW1V 2SA

A CIP catalogue record for this book
is available from the British Library

ISBN 0–224–02757–3

Typeset by J&L Composition Ltd, Filey, North Yorkshire
Printed by Mackays of Chatham PLC

For David Lloyd
of Wernant
with llove

ONE

ONCE IN THE green valley Owen Tudor kept his grassy farm. In it lived Owen himself, Gwen his wife, David his son, and Myfanwy his daughter.

There were geese, there were sheep, there were black cows, licking their noses. There were speckled pigs, there was Angharad the grey horse, and Delyth the brown one, there was Marged the oldest donkey in the world, and there were Bess and Lyart, the two dogs.

Down at the pond there were ducks, around the farmhouse there were fourteen hens and a cockerel, and some scuffling rats, which nobody wanted except the farm cats, and in the orchard two hives of bees, which nobody counted.

Round the chimneys of the house fluttered white doves that Myfanwy had made tame. David thought of sending messages with them, if anyone wanted to hear.

They all lived among the green fields. Each day Owen would see family and fields and know they were all there. He would shake his head at the rats, and listen to see that the bees were happy.

"These are what I want," said Owen to himself, leaning on a gate, or whistling as he milked. "This makes me wealthy enough."

Then he would walk in his own fields. Before there were Englishmen in England there were Tudors in this valley. The fields had belonged to his father before him, and to his father's father before that.

Or perhaps, thought Owen, we all belonged to the fields, and shall do so for ever. Half my heart is here, I know.

But the other half was in the farmhouse just below the little wood there.

"More than half my heart is here, all at the same time," thought Owen to himself.

So he would finish his milking, or his work in a field, and go home to his supper.

And so it had been, right away back from the time of the fairies, long ago, when the Tudors came to the valley. Owen Tudor, or Emrys Tudor, or David Tudor (Owen, or his father, or his grandfather), whoever was the farmer, would finish his day's work and go home contented.

Until, one day, a little black van came into the valley, and stopped beside the shop, the Swyddfa'r Post.

"They have lost their way," said David Tudor. "They will be English tourists."

"Or perhaps they are looking for a dog for the film studio," said Myfanwy. "They will want a girl to look after the dog also."

"It is nothing," said Owen.

"I am dishing up the tea," said Gwen, in the kitchen. "The van will be gone tomorrow, and they will tell us at the Swyddfa'r Post."

"The gossip will last a week," said Owen.

But the gossip was going to last for ever, yet for a long time no one knew what it was about.

There were two men in the van. They stayed the night at Mrs Morgan Jones's bed and breakfast, but they were not tourists.

In the morning they went for a walk, but they were not interested in the scenery. Grandpa Morgan Jones took his beard and his pipe up the street to them, but they were not interested in history. He always told everyone about working for seventy-five years at the slate quarry up the valley. "It is an art," he would say, "slate cutting."

"Strange," said Gwen.

"The whole world has heard the history of Grandpa Morgan Jones," said Owen. "They do not want to hear it again, slate by slate."

The two men walked in every field. They had little notebooks. Grandpa Morgan Jones thought that school slates were all that was necessary. Myfanwy thought the notebooks might be drawing books, but when she saw into one she did not understand the drawings.

"They never saw anything like that," she said. But she did not know what maps were. The men told her to run away and not trouble them any more. They were quite polite, but said it in English.

They did not tell her what the notebooks were for. They did not tell anyone. They told each other in long words, worse than English.

"They are looking at our little pasture," said Owen. "Not eating much grass, but looking hungry, all the same. I shall ask them what they want."

But when he had come to the little pasture the men were behind the wood, and when he was behind the wood they had gone down to the long meadow, and when Owen was at the high end of the meadow they were at the low end. So he came home.

9

"No, they will think I am inquisitive," he said. "So I am, perhaps, but I do not want them to know. But I do want to know why they are looking, looking."

"It isn't at our dogs," said Myfanwy.

"Quite true," said David. "They do not look at the animals."

"They are not looking at the grass on the ground," said Owen. "It doesn't trouble them at all."

"Or at the buildings and houses," said Gwen. "When they came by the gate I asked whether they would like a cup of tea, because I had just drawn water from the well, but they smiled and smiled and went by."

"That is that," said Owen. "They will be gone. Grandpa Morgan Jones told me they will stay one more night only, breakfast but no dinner, so they're off in the morning."

But the men and their little black van chose the wrong way to go, if they were in a hurry. Owen did not know what they were doing at all. Nobody did. So it was a matter of luck that he and David, with Myfanwy and the dogs helping them, were driving some calves along the lane after breakfast.

The calves saw the black van coming towards them and did not know what it was. They were more afraid of the van than they were of Owen and David and Myfanwy, and forgot they had bad dreams about dogs. So the calves tramped round in a circle in the middle of the lane, Owen shouted and waved a stick, David tried to push, Myfanwy called to them to come on, and the dogs scratched their ears.

The men opened the doors of the van and got out. They thought they were being helpful. But the calves knew it was time to go home, and that was where they went, skid, thump, bellow, rolling of eyes.

"We are sorry," said one of the men.

"Never mind," said Owen. "You go on by and we'll fetch them down again. David, Myfanwy, take the dogs and bring the calves down once more, but wait until the van has gone, see."

"We have to explain if the van is scratched," said the other man. "It belongs to the Water Board."

"Water Board?" said Owen. "What is that? Surfing?"

"The people who take water to Birmingham," said the first man. "We're looking for water, of course."

"Water?" said Owen. "Birmingham? In Birmingham you can turn a tap and it pours out. You would be better off at home. Our water is better, but we have to get it from the well. Are you about to give us some taps, modern, like?"

"Nothing like that," said the first man.

"Does the van need a bucket of water?" asked Owen. "I will go up at once and bring it, and a second one if it is not enough."

"A bucket or two will not be enough," said the second man. "We are looking for enough water for Birmingham, because sometimes there is nothing in the taps."

"Our well has never dried," said Owen, proudly. The men nodded their heads. Owen knew he had said the right thing. But at the same time he knew he had said the wrong one.

"We shall want all there is," said the first man.

"We can fill buckets for you," said Owen, but he knew that was not quite what the men wanted.

"Buckets are not enough, Mr Tudor," said the second man.

11

"I see Grandpa Morgan Jones has told you all the names," said Owen.

"We knew all the names," said the first man. "But about the buckets. No, that is not how it is done. The water will go to Birmingham in a big pipe, a hundred miles. We shall fill the pipe from a big lake."

"There is only the village pond," said Owen.

"We shall build a dam," said the second man. "We shall fill the whole valley with water."

"But what about the fields?" said Owen. "This land has belonged to the Tudor family so long no one can remember. You cannot drown our farms. And of course you cannot, because I will never sell it to you, not if you offered me ten times its value. Ten times."

"It has been decided," said both men, one after the other. "Now they are bringing your cows down again, so we shall drive on out of your way. Good morning."

"But I have not finished," said Owen. He had though, because the van want on past him, and there was no one to speak to.

"Cows indeed," said Owen Tudor. "Just some young bullocks. They do not understand farming at Birmingham."

TWO

"IF I HAD known what they were doing, the wickeds," said Mrs Morgan Jones, "they would never have stayed in my bed and breakfast."

A lot of people were standing in front of the building called Swyddfa'r Post, which means Post Office. David was skimming stones across the pond, and Myfanwy was telling him not to frighten the real ducks and drakes.

"Wicked is right, you'll see," said Postman Griffith, coming out of the office with his bag on his shoulder. "There are letters for all of us today, Mrs Morgan Jones. Owen Tudor, shall I give you yours now and save me the walk?"

"And what about me?" said Grandpa Morgan Jones.

"One in the bottom of the bag for you," said Postman Griffith. "Up here you are all having the same letter, and people are getting very cross about it, I can tell you, so I'll be on my way."

Before he went he handed out more and more letters. Some people had more than one, perhaps from their auntie, or a friend, or even a bill from the grocery. But everybody had one letter, and all were the same except the name and address.

Postman Griffith was right. Everybody was cross. Some of them tore their letters up and dropped them on the muddy edge of the pond.

But in the end they picked them up, wiped the mud off, and took them home.

They said at the top: CITY OF BIRMINGHAM WATER SUPPLY, which was not friendly. Then they went on to talk about what was going to happen, and to say that money would be given to everybody.

Owen Tudor explained to Gwen. "They will build a dam," he said. "They are making a reservoir, and the valley will be a big lake."

"We shall be able to catch fish," said David.

"But where is the lake going to be built?" asked Gwen. "They take up a lot of space."

"Here," said Owen. "Right on top of our farm, all over our fields."

"All over the village," said Mrs Morgan Jones. "Drowning bed and breakfast, house and all."

"All for the English in Birmingham," said Grandpa Morgan Jones. "I went there on the train once, and it is a dirty place, the station. If they are short of water why can't they be short of someone else's, and leave us alone?"

But there was no arguing about it. All the letters said the same thing, that the valley would be filled with water.

"I shall never sell," said Owen. "Not for a hundred times what the land is worth. Never."

But Grandpa Morgan Jones shook his beard a great deal and said that was not likely.

"It would make no difference if they did, is what I said," Owen explained. "The land has never been bought with money. The first Tudor, and they say he was a giant, built the house with his own hands, digging out the stone from the hillside. It is our house right through."

"That was in the time of the fairies," said Grandpa Morgan Jones. "Now it is the English."

No one replied to the letters. No one wanted money for their houses. All of them would rather have house and land and a quiet valley.

There were more letters. Birmingham wrote to the valley, even if the valley would not write to it. One day Postman Griffith brought Owen a letter saying that the farm did not belong to him any more, but there was money waiting for him in a bank.

"Do not blame me," said Postman Griffith. "There is a meeting tonight about it at the bed and breakfast. Mind how you go. When I drove up this morning in the red van the machines were beginning work."

Owen Tudor went to the meeting. Everybody who owned a house was there. Grandpa Morgan Jones was put by the window to be rid of his pipe smoke. The noise of machinery came in as the smoke went out.

"Everything has been taken from us," said Mrs Morgan Jones. "I have looked at all the letters. They have taken everything that belonged to all of us, and we shall have to go."

"Every bit," said someone else, "every stick of hedge, every yard of road, every acre we owned, every stone of each wall, all gone. Stolen, I say, stolen."

"And closing the slate quarry," said Grandpa Morgan Jones. "People are needing slates just as much as ever, keep out the rain. The Saeson will be drowned in their beds from rain." Saeson is what the Welsh call the English.

15

"I can tell you," said Goronwy from the next farm, "we shall be drowned in our fields if we do not move out. Marching orders we have got, left right, left right. Nothing here for us now, nothing."

"Just one thing they forgot, and which I remember from being a boy," said Grandpa Morgan Jones. No one wanted to listen to him in case he began on his life story.

"Go in the kitchen, put on the kettle again," said Mrs Morgan Jones. "Go on, Grandpa."

"They have thought of everything," said Owen. "But all the same they do not care."

"They have not thought of everything," said Grandpa Morgan Jones, shaking his head, sitting firmly where he was, puffing black smoke. He wanted to be heard.

"Well, what is it, Grandpa?" said Mrs Morgan Jones. "Tell us the big thing."

"They have forgotten the duckpond," said Grandpa Morgan Jones, "because it does not belong to anyone. That is all."

"It is not much," said Mrs Morgan Jones. "We can forget about it too. Duckpond indeed, typical useless wisdom. Do what I ask, there's a good Grandpa, put the kettle on, be so kind."

"There is a reason for it," said Grandpa. "I will remember before long, and it will not be so useless. I know about the duckpond."

"The whole valley will be a duckpond before long," said Owen, "and none of it will belong to us. Well, if that is all, I shall go home without waiting for tea. It will just remind me of the water it is made from."

He went home. He was very gloomy, and no one

dared speak to him. Gwen cooked the best supper, and David and Myfanwy helped with the farm. Even the two dogs kept quiet and the cows peaceful.

Owen Tudor went to bed that night early. All the same, he did not sleep. He lay awake and watched the moonlight on the window. Now and then he sighed to himself and turned over to look at the wallpaper on the wall, or sat up and looked at the foot of the bed.

"Owen, Owen, why are you so restless?" asked Gwen, because the bedclothes were all over the place.

"You know what is on my mind," said Owen. "We shall have to leave and start again with nothing."

"We shall have the animals," said Gwen. "Only the land will be different. You can be the first Tudor to settle somewhere else, and in a thousand years they will look back to you as the first of all the Tudors."

"It is easy to say, Gwen," said Owen. "But it is not good."

"Now, other people have done it," said Gwen. "Look, in the chapel last Sunday we were talking about Abraham setting off for a new place with only his flocks and herds."

"Well," said Owen, feeling too tired to argue, but still no nearer sleep, "I am sorry for Abraham, indeed, and that is all."

And he looked out of the window this time, at his fields all white in the moonlight. One day they would be flooded, he thought, and what a bad day that would be.

Then all at once another thought came into his mind, almost like something crawling up his back suddenly. "Well," he said to himself. Then, "Gwen, surely Abraham is not the only person mentioned in the Bible?"

"Indeed not," said Gwen. "Have you forgotten?"

"No," said Owen. "I have remembered. I have remembered. And now I think I can go to sleep."

"I hope so," said Gwen, gathering back her share of bedclothes.

"You see, I know what to do," said Owen. "It is all perfectly clear and simple. So perfectly clear and simple."

But instead of explaining it he went to sleep, and Gwen did not hear what it was.

"It is too simple for me, then," she said to herself, and went to sleep as well, Owen snoring gently, allowing her a share of the covers.

In the morning she did not ask, and Owen did not say anything. Gwen thought he had forgotten.

"Perhaps he was asleep without meaning it," she thought. "But he has something in mind, I know him. He is not unhappy any more; he has decided. But what it is I do not know."

She looked at him eating his breakfast, and decided he was a happy man, considering how he had worried so.

And Owen thought he was a happy man too, considering what he was about to do.

THREE

WHEN THE MORNING'S work was done, the cows milked, turnips chopped for the sheep, the donkey given some hay, Owen came in for a cup of tea.

"And a clean shirt," he said, "and my town trousers and my market jacket, Gwen, be so good."

"It is not market day," said Gwen.

"I know that," said Owen. "But I cannot wait until then. What I have to do is urgent, now, today. While you are getting them ready I shall harness Angharad and Delyth, and put them to the big cart, because I am buying a great deal of stuff."

"Indeed," said Gwen, putting down the kettle so that she could wag a finger at him. "Where are you getting money, Owen Tudor?"

"From Birmingham," said Owen. "Haven't they sent a lot to the bank? That is the money. I will spend it, but not in a way they expect. You will see. So stop wagging at me, my girl."

Gwen stopped wagging. She put the kettle on. Owen hitched both horses to the big cart, and came in to drink his tea, wash and shave, and put on town clothes.

"We shall have to go to market soon to sell the animals," said Gwen. "I shall do a big shopping for winter."

"You shall do the biggest shopping in the world," said Owen. "But as for selling the animals, well, that is another story." He gave Gwen a big kiss to cheer her up, because she was quite puzzled by him, and went off down the lane.

"If I meet a little black van," said Owen, "then, boyo, Angharad will put her foot through the roof, and Delyth will put hers through the motor, and we will trample it. The men will run back all the way to Birmingham, and welcome."

"Drive carefully," said Gwen, watching him out of sight.

She watched anxiously for him. She hoped he was not going to Birmingham himself to trample on vans. She hoped the policeman would not come telling her there was trouble. She just wished, while she did her washing, that Owen would come back safe, and tell her what he was doing.

"It is not a wishing well," she sighed, as she drew water from it for her laundry.

Owen came back late, and very slow. He was so long coming that when they came in from school David and Myfanwy milked the cows and foddered all the animals. Then Gwen put a pie in the oven, and they waited for Owen to come in and cut it.

It was dark when they heard the cart. It was coming heavily past Mrs Morgan Jones's bed and breakfast, past the Swyddfa'r Post, past Grandpa Morgan Jones's little cottage, full of wood fresh cut from the timber merchant. It was not only full, it was heaped up too. Angharad and Delyth were pulling, pulling, all the way, and Owen walked beside them, pulling with them.

"They will never get up the hill to the farmyard," said Gwen. "We shall have to go and help push."

So they all went down and met Owen by the pond, where he seemed to be having a rest.

"Oh, there you are," he said. "I was looking for you. David, go and open the bottom gate there and I shall take the cart into the bottom pasture."

"There is too much on it to get to the house," said Grandpa Morgan Jones, waving his pipe and knowing all about everything.

"That is not the question," said Owen. "I only wish to go into my bottom pasture by the pond. So away with you, David, open the gate."

"I suppose you know what you are doing," said Grandpa Morgan Jones. "But I never saw anything like it in my life, which is ninety-seven years."

"And not a bit too long, Grandpa," said Owen. "Just give a push at the tail of the cart to get her going, and we'll be off."

Angharad and Delyth bent their knees and pulled, many people pushed at the back, and the cart went past the pond and into the pasture.

It stood there that night. Owen shut the gate behind it, unhitched the horses, and brought them back to their stable.

"The children will see to them," said Gwen. "Owen, you will tell me what you are doing; and then we shall have our pie."

"I am looking forward to pie," said Owen.

But what he was doing with such a lot of wood in the bottom pasture he would not say.

"I do not want it to get about," he said. "It is a secret. People may think and think, but until they know it does not matter. I shall not say a word. Even

Angharad and Delyth do not know, and as for that old Morgan Jones, well, we know better than to think of anything at all anywhere near him. It is gossip in a second. He even talks to hikers, and got too much to tell in any case."

"We shall wait and see, in that case," said Gwen, "Now all that fetching and carrying is done."

Owen shook his head. "Fetching and carrying haven't started yet," he said. "That's today, but there's tomorrow, and tomorrow, and the day after that. I am going to be busy."

He had been so busy already that the pie was not quite enough, and the dish was scraped out much sooner than usual.

"You will have to use a bigger dish," said Owen, carrying it to the sink and letting it float there. "Never mind, today I shall fill up with bread and cheese. I warn you, I shall be a hungry man."

But, no matter how much Gwen made him special puddings, or how much Myfanwy sat on his knee and made him laugh, no matter how much David said, "Come on, Da, tell us; I won't tell the girls"; no matter that Mrs Morgan Jones said, "Come on, tell me straight, Owen Tudor"; no matter that Postman Griffith brought envelopes thick with bills, Owen went on with what he was doing without explaining it to anyone.

He went each day, except Sunday, down to the town. He came back each day with a new load of wood and placed it carefully in the bottom pasture, each load exactly in a certain place.

"That's the way," he said. "All worked out." He unloaded the cart each time, turned it round, and went down with it empty the next day.

And still the life of the farm went on, with animals being milked and fed, eggs collected, firewood cut, all the work continuing as usual. But on neighbouring farms the animals were being sold off and the people were moving out.

"That is their affair," said Owen. "I am not going anywhere at the moment, am I? So I am not saying goodbye. That would be ridiculous."

And when neighbours came to say goodbye to him he would tell them they were wrong to give in. But he would not say what he was doing.

"But I'll gladly say goodbye to Grandpa Morgan Jones," he said. "Always scheming, these last hundred years, nearly. Born with that inquisitive beard and that talkative pipe, him."

And away down below the village the machinery was working day and night, building a huge thick wall across the valley. The little river still ran down freely, but now it went through a gate in the dam. When the time came the gate would close, the river would no longer escape and the valley would begin to fill.

Owen saw the building each day as he went past to the town. One market day, when he took Gwen down, a tear dropped from the end of her nose when she saw what was happening.

"Hush now," said Owen, "it isn't happening to you."

"It is happening to the valley," said Gwen.

Owen paid his bills. He would not let Gwen know how much the wood cost, but she knew it must be a great deal because he once had to ask her about the noughts in a thousand for the longest sum he had ever done.

The carrier brought him boxes from far away. The heaviest came from Birmingham, and everybody saw it because the man had to ask the way at the Swyddfa'r Post, and there was the word painted on the box.

"Leave it in the bottom pasture," said Grandpa Morgan Jones. "Birmingham indeed. He cannot get any good from there. What is he thinking about?"

Owen would not tell. But he thanked Grandpa Morgan Jones for his advice to the man. "It is just where I wanted it," he said.

The inside was full of bolts, nuts, screws, nails, rods, clamps, turnscrews, buckles, bits, drills, clouts, hold-fasts, cramps, plates and flitches, all black and new, all warm from the factory. On top of all was a very firm padlock and chain.

"Most essential," said Owen. "What's locked away can't be seen by peering eyes."

"I thought it might have been 'baccy in the box," said Grandpa Morgan Jones. "I know what that's for."

"And I know what this is for," said Owen, locking and unlocking the padlock.

But no one else knew what the lock was for.

"Not a word out of him," said Gwen at the Swyddfa'r Post one day. "If he had said I daresay he would forbid me to tell, so I don't see how you can be a penny the wiser."

"Men," said Mrs Morgan Jones. "No wonder there is gossip."

"There," said Gwen. "And when are you leaving, Mrs Morgan Jones?"

"Oh, last thing," said Mrs Morgan Jones. "Trade is good just now, and trade is money. I have ten bed and breakfast gentlemen now, all working on the dam, bringing in good wages."

"Buying plenty of bacon and sausages," said the Swyddfa'r Post lady.

"Got to keep their strength up, working so hard," said Mrs Morgan Jones. "Nice lads, too. Pity what they are doing is so wicked, isn't it?"

Gwen went home cross about that. "They are all traitors," she said. "We do not want the dam built."

"No," said David.

"Indeed not," said Myfanwy. "All my friends have gone already."

"We've got to have the dam now," said Owen, thoughtfully. "My plan isn't any use without it, so why not make money from them?"

But he still would not explain the plan. All he said was that the very next day he was not going to the town, because he was starting work in the bottom pasture.

FOUR

WORK IN THE bottom pasture usually meant cutting the thistles, or taking some nuts to the lambs, or spreading rich smelly stuff over the grass. That would make Mrs Morgan Jones's nose wrinkle, but Grandpa felt it added flavour to his pipe. And the grass would grow.

The work was different now. Owen first set up a row of posts, measuring the places for the holes. Then he set up another. Grandpa Morgan Jones stood at the Swyddfa'r Post side of the pond and looked up between the rows.

"Building a railway," he said. "Is that it, Tudor?"

Owen took no notice. When he had dug some more holes and set up some more posts he had an oblong marked out.

"Bowling green," said Grandpa Morgan Jones. "When I was young I played that, but the English built the balls crooked inside, typical."

Still Owen said nothing. He measured the work he had done. Some of the wood was used for the posts, but all the rest was inside the rectangle.

Grandpa Morgan Jones waited to see what happened next. Mrs Morgan Jones waited. Postman Griffith waited. The bed and breakfast gentlemen looked up the street from their beds and breakfasts to see what was to be done. Gwen looked down, David and Myfanwy came to see close-to.

"I am the only one that knows," said Owen.

The ducks and geese came to investigate. If they found out they said nothing that could be understood.

The next part of Owen's plan was a roof over what he had built. He sloped it in from all the sides, and then nailed corrugated iron on, so that there was a building in the pasture.

The man from the Council wrote and told him to take it down.

"That'll make him mad," said Grandpa Morgan Jones. Postman Griffith had not liked to take him the letter, guessing what was in it. Gwen had not liked to take it into the house.

"I do not know what he will say," she said.

"I will be off," said Postman Griffith. "In case he does."

Owen said, "I like letters," and threw it on the fire without looking at it. He went back to the building and finished the roof. Then he made Grandpa Morgan Jones mad by building up all the sides of the building until no one could see in. And on the door he left for himself he put the very large padlock, so that no one could know anything at all.

Grandpa Morgan Jones's beard twitched all on its own. "We have a right to know," he said.

"Sit down, Grandpa," said Mrs Morgan Jones.

The man from the Council came himself to tell Owen to take the building down. Everyone waited for trouble, some with glee (Grandpa Morgan Jones), some with anxiety (Mrs Morgan Jones), some with a

27

knowing shake of the head (Postman Griffith), some with dread (Gwen and Myfanwy), and some in the hope of a fight (David). And one kept his strong bowler hat on his head just in case (the man from the Council).

"Of course," said Owen, quite peacefully and happily, when he heard the news. "Come in, man, and have a cup of tea. Gwen, make the man a pot of tea, and I'll have a cup myself. But I can't take it down yet, because, you see, I haven't finished it yet. Now have some curranty cake, spread plenty of butter on it, that's right."

"I understand," said the man. "I see you can't take it down until it's there. Yes, another cup would be lovely, Mrs Tudor, and perhaps another dab of butter would be nice. But don't take too long, because I have to report back to the Council. In the meantime perhaps I'd just better tell them the purpose of the building, what it's for, eh?"

"It's there to be taken down when it's finished," said Owen. "That is the truth."

When the man had gone, taking a section of cake with him and several cups of tea, Gwen asked Owen what he meant.

"You have never told me anything either," she said. "I don't know any better than the Council."

"I have not told either of you one word of a lie," said Owen.

Down in the village everyone was disappointed at not being right about anything. Grandpa Morgan Jones bought all the 'baccy in the Swyddfa'r Post and packed it in a bag. When he left, he said, he might not find another shop.

But Owen found another shop, or provision

28

merchant. He bought hay by the wagonload. He bought grain by the truck. He sent for flour by the sack, sugar by the barrel, ham by the whole pig-full. All day long, it seemed, vans and carts were coming up. And all of them stopped in the bottom pasture, and were unloaded by Owen himself, no helpers allowed.

In between deliveries he went on working inside the building, hammering, sawing, drilling, knocking things into shape.

He bought a whole railway wagon of coal and shovelled that in. He sent for crates of currants, for chests of tea, for hotel-size jars of pickle.

"Going to live in it," said Grandpa Jones. "The roof will let the rain in like it wasn't really there, and that'll be a pudding." And his beard laughed to itself. "What do you think you are doing, Tudor?"

Owen, far inside the building, drove a great nail in, wham, bang, slam. But nothing shut Grandpa up.

One day Mrs Morgan Jones began to take her curtains down. "The working gentlemen are going," she told Owen. "The dam is built and they are off to another one."

"Some other poor valley somewhere," said Gwen. "But I hear some people got quite rich on the bed and breakfast business."

"Mustn't grumble beyond necessary," said Mrs Morgan Jones. "My, doesn't the place look bare without curtains?"

"It will look worse without people," said Gwen. But when she told Owen that, he told her not to be silly, but would not say what the silly was. All the same, he gave her a kiss for being thoughtful.

The dam was now quite finished. People could

walk right along the top of it, and indeed the view was lovely both up and down the valley.

Down the valley the river no longer flowed. The gates had been shut and no water got through.

Up the valley the river was filling the bottom of the dam and stretching back up its bed, almost to the village, wider and deeper, covering green fields already, drowning trees, and making the rabbits sit about in the bottoms of hedges wondering what was going on.

"Who would think we could be up here," said Gwen, looking down from the top with Myfanwy, helping Mrs Morgan Jones take a last look before she was off with curtains and beds and breakfasts. "Look, there is your Da."

"I can see him," said Myfanwy. "But I do not understand what he is doing."

When she had looked too Gwen did not understand either. Mrs Morgan Jones shook her head and went back to pack her ornaments.

The time of year was the beginning of winter, Christmas not far away, cold weather coming, and all the cows were indoors until spring. They had been indoors several weeks.

But now Owen was driving them all out of their shippon and into the fields. The two dogs, Bess and Lyart, were helping.

"Not even a sunny day," said Gwen. "In fact getting dark. And there's not a scrap of grass to eat until it grows again."

"Da will know, perhaps," said Myfanwy.

"I am wondering," said Gwen. "We had better go back and see."

When they got back Owen knew perfectly well

what he was doing. "Cows like a bit of change," he said. "They're down in the new building. That's their place now."

"But I thought you were going to take it down," said Gwen. "You told the Council man that you would."

"I shall," said Owen. "It's nearly finished. You know I can't start before that."

And a couple of days later, when the water of the river was beginning to look into the garden of the Swyddfa'r Post, Owen came to his house and said that the work was done.

"David, harness up Angharad and Delyth and bring them to the bottom pasture. Gwen, go down to the village and bring back as many people as you can. Myfanwy, put the kettle on and butter some cake, because they will need it when they have done. I will go and catch the donkey, because she has work to do as well."

Everybody came from the village, Postman Griffith included, and the ten young gentlemen from the bed and breakfast, popping back with a present for Mrs Morgan Jones. Grandpa Morgan Jones wanted his cup of tea before he began whatever it was they had come to do.

"His beard is hungry," said David, and gave him Angharad to hold instead.

"There now," said Grandpa Morgan Jones, "I understand horses, don't I, boyo?"

Angharad bit his beard, and Delyth trod on his foot. "Love them," said Grandpa.

"Now what are we to do?" said Postman Griffith. "This is my last trip here, Owen. Your address does not exist any more after today, off the map it is, so there is no delivery, and the Swyddfa'r Post is closed from mid-day, and they are blocking off the road at four o'clock."

"It is the last day of the village," said Owen. "But there is not going to be a last day of the Tudor farm, because there are places off the map but still in the world. Now you, Griffith, and you, Morgan Jones, and some of you lads, lift the bars that hold the end of the building just by the pond, and take it away to one side. I will show you what I have made, and you will understand."

Someone else came squelching through the mud, carrying a notebook, raising his bowler hat to the ladies present, nodding to Grandpa Morgan Jones, smiling at children and ducks, and looking severely at Owen.

"About this building, Mr Tudor," he said. "The Council has instructed me to . . ."

"Just blink your eyes once or twice," said Owen. "In four minutes' time there will be no building, just as I told you. If the Council wants it to be true then lay hold of the peen end of that building and lift when I say. Go on, put your notebook away."

". . . say that on no account . . ." said the man from the Council. Then he had to stop, because the building was waiting to be taken down, and he had to agree that was what he wanted.

Postman Griffith, Grandpa Morgan Jones, four of the bed and breakfast gentlemen, and the man in his bowler hat, picked their way through mud and water to the building. The river had by now backed up to the pond and begun to fill it, so they paddled through its overflow.

"All together now," said Owen. "Take it to one side. I shall need it later."

"You've got something heavy there," said Grandpa Morgan Jones, getting beard and pipe on the job.

"Heave," said the beds, and "Ho," said the breakfasts.

"Steady," said Owen.

"Mind the ducks," said Myfanwy, because they were dabbling in new waters for fresh worms.

"Mind the drakes," said David, dancing about with excitement and skimming stones across the same new waters.

"One, two," said Postman Griffith, "three, four, Mary at the cottage door."

The end of the building came away and was carried off, showing what was inside the building, what Owen had been making.

"I understand," said Gwen. "Of course, there were more people than Abraham in the Bible, and I know which one you meant. You are perfectly clever, Owen."

And, "You'll never get it off the ground," said Grandpa Morgan Jones.

FIVE

THERE WAS SILENCE for a moment or two. Even the ducks stopped quacking and looked at the thing in the building.

"It's pointed," said Mrs Morgan Jones, at last, not understanding in the least what Owen had built.

"That's an airship," said Grandpa Morgan Jones. "Tudor, you can't drive one of them, you'll be bringing down churches and town halls and railway stations and you'll drop anchor on the electric and go up in smoke." His idea was not very clear either. But he wagged his knowing little beard, sure he was right.

But Owen was grinning at Gwen, glad she understood, beaming at everyone else, even Grandpa Morgan Jones, smiling at Mrs Morgan Jones, longing to see her understand at last; but that wasn't going to be until he told her.

"But Owen," said Gwen, when she caught his happy eye again, "this is all very clever, and right, I know. But where are we going in it?"

"Gwen, Gwen," said Owen, letting his smiles and beams fade, "you have not understood. Have I done all this for you not to understand?"

"I understand," said Gwen. "We talked about

34

Abraham, and his flocks and herds, setting off for a new place, with his cows and his sheep and the old donkey, see. But you have done better, and still stayed with a Bible story. You have built an Ark, like Noah, and that is brilliant."

"Ark?" said Grandpa Morgan Jones.

"Live in it?" said Mrs Morgan Jones, quite startled. "Bed and breakfast?"

"No lodgers," said Gwen. "Just family."

"Lodgers indeed," said Mrs Morgan Jones. "Gentlemen, I had, see them."

"The Council", said their man, getting his notebook out again, "will want to know about this."

Grandpa Morgan Jones stroked his beard, which had gone limp with despair. "Never told a soul," he said. "But I daresay you built an airship by accident, easy to do if you don't understand the plans."

"I've been longing to say for years," said Owen, "Grandpa Morgan Jones, go jump in the lake, be so good. But don't go yet, I want some more beard-power a minute. Just let me settle with Gwen here. And if your gentlemen don't mind waiting a moment as well, Mrs Morgan Jones; and David and Myfanwy, just get the horses hitched to the rings on the front of the Ark."

"Now, there's a right way to do it," said Grandpa Morgan Jones, who would not be beaten at anything and certainly was not jumping in the lake. He went off with the horses and David and Myfanwy.

"Get the long ropes out too," said Owen to the bed and breakfasters. "You'll see them." Then he turned to Gwen.

She was looking at him, still puzzled.

"There'll be plenty of room for us," she said. "But

35

where are we going? The river has been blocked up now, and that thing is so big it would hardly go down it in any case. And wherever it is, we could have gone in wagons like the other farmers."

"My love," said Owen, "you haven't understood. I expect Noah had the same problem with Mrs Noah."

"She got shipwrecked on the mountains," said Gwen. "I remember from Sunday School, the mountains of Ararat, right on top, hit a rock."

"A church tower, a railway station," said Grandpa Morgan Jones. "That's what it'll be."

"But he didn't set out for there," said Owen. "Drifted, he did, didn't know any better. But you and me, we're not going anywhere. We're staying here."

Mrs Morgan Jones shook her head. "But you can't stay on your land, Owen. The water people of Birmingham have taken it from you."

"You got the money instead," said Gwen. "And you spent that."

"No," said Owen, "I got no land, I know. You don't have an Ark on land. When you've built it you put it on the water."

"But the way it is," said Mrs Morgan Jones, "the land goes right up to the sky, so when it gets flooded with the dam it still isn't yours to go on."

"I know that too," said Owen. "You are a pack of simpletons. Even old Grandpa Morgan Jones knows what I am talking about, pipe and beard and all."

"You talking about me, Tudor?" said Grandpa Morgan Jones. "We've got all fast here. What next?"

"Something you said was right," said Owen.

"Well?" said Grandpa. "So? What's wrong with that?"

"Everything, I daresay," said Mrs Morgan Jones.

"But go on, Owen. All this I have to hear. Tell us all."

"Right," said Owen. "This Ark will float."

"That remains to be seen," said Grandpa Morgan Jones.

". . . Will float," said Owen. "So all we have to do is get it to the water."

"The water will come to it," said one of the beds.

"Rising a foot a day," said a breakfast. "Two metres a week. Exponentially," or some such strange word.

"That is over the land that has been stolen from us," said Owen. "But, you see, they forgot to buy the pond from us, because they thought it didn't belong to anyone. So we get that Ark on the pond, which is why I built it just here, and there it will stay."

"You'll get drowned when the water covers you," said Mrs Morgan Jones. "Oh no you won't, because you will rise up on the water, and it still stays part of the pond no matter how high it rises."

"It won't ride higher than the top of the dam," said a bed.

"Not designed to, at any rate," said a breakfast.

"They know it all," said Mrs Morgan Jones.

Grandpa Morgan Jones was looking very pleased with himself for having given Owen the idea, and also rather alarmed. "I never meant," he said.

"You didn't know you gave me anything," said Owen. "Now Gwen, do you understand what I mean? We shall stay just here, in the valley, and not go away at all."

Gwen shook her head, but not in disagreement. It was because she had misunderstood. "I did not doubt you," she said. "But you did not tell me so I did not know. But now I think you have got the better of them all, and we must get the Ark on the pond before anything goes wrong. I will pull a rope, or two ropes, and we shall get it done."

It took them until dark, and a bit beyond, before horses, donkey, beds and breakfasts, Grandpa Morgan Jones, Mrs Morgan Jones, the lady from the Swyddfa'r Post, Postman Griffith, and all the Tudor family, had dragged the Ark out of the building and slid it on to the pond.

The Ark did not come out of the building in the way that anyone there expected. First the end of the building came off, which was when they first saw the Ark inside. But most of the roof was part of the Ark, and so were parts of the sides, up towards the middle.

Owen went along taking away pieces that were only building and laying them in the field. There were not many, just the front end in one piece, parts of the back end, because that was straight up, like a building end, and parts of the sides. And those parts folded up to make a rail round the decks of the Ark.

"I said I would take it down," said Owen. "I have kept all my promises. Now pull, boys, pull you good girls."

"He is talking to the horses," said Gwen. "Not you and me, Mrs Morgan Jones."

Inch by inch the Ark came, sliding across the soft field. The first end of it was the bows, all shining wood. On top was a deck, and there were holes for an anchor rope, and an anchor waiting to be dropped.

"If Noah had anchored he would have stayed home," said Owen. "I shall anchor in the pond, and make the rope longer as the water gets deeper. I have it all worked out, because we know how deep the water will be."

"Am I pushing all alone?" came a cry from Grandpa Morgan Jones, at the stern of the Ark.

"Doing good work, Grandpa," Owen shouted. "Don't stop."

No one stopped. They all pulled, or pushed, in silence. The beds and breakfasts started a song, but soon gave up. Above the song there came another noise, which was the bellowing of cows.

"What is the matter with them?" asked Gwen.

"Keep pulling," said Owen.

"Something is the matter," said Gwen.

"Their shippon is moving about," said Owen.

"Why is that?" asked Gwen. "Oh, yes, of course, the cows are aboard already. Are all our animals coming, Owen, as well as us?"

"That is the meaning of an Ark," said Owen. "Taking all the animals aboard, only we've got several of a few kinds, not just two of all kinds."

"So we don't get to live in all of it," said Gwen.

"No, we are sharing," said Owen.

"Not sharing too close, I hope," said Gwen. "People in their place, animals in theirs, I say, Owen."

But just then the front of the Ark touched the pond and rippled the water. At the far end Grandpa Morgan Jones went face down and got mud in his beard.

A long time after that the front of the Ark touched the far side of the pond. This time Grandpa Morgan Jones had his pipe filled with bubbles.

The stern of the Ark slid down the bank, and the

Ark itself floated. There was a foot to spare at each end.

"I measured it," said Owen. "It doesn't overhang at all. There could be a case against me if it did. But here we are on the pond, and it's too late for them to turn us off. So now come aboard, because when the water rises it won't be so simple to visit us."

The way aboard was over the stern. The spare pieces of building made a ramp it was easy to walk up, and everyone came, except the bed and breakfast gentlemen, who had to go into town, where they now lodged.

Owen's promise was kept. There was now no trace of the building in the bottom pasture. But there was a large trace of an Ark on the pond.

"It has worked," he said. "It is perfect. I knew it would be so."

"It will not be perfect," said Grandpa Morgan Jones. "Tudor, I have something to tell you."

Gwen was going about with a torch in the dark, peering through doorways and creeping along passages.

"Not much space," she said. "All these rooms are full. This would make a nice sitting-room, Owen, but it is full of hay; and I would like to sew in here, but it is full of straw. And the children's bedrooms, one is full of flour, and David's is full of boxes and barrels."

"Provisions," said Owen. "You are down in the farm. We shall live on top, see, in here." And he showed her the cabins above the decks. "Kitchen," he said. "Here is the stove when we get it out of the house, and here the old clock will stand, and in this room our chairs will be, and there the table, because I have made it just the same as home, because home is where we are."

And he had even put the same wallpaper on the walls, and the same rugs on the floor. Only the furniture was needed to complete the house.

"And I built a bathroom on, so we don't need the tub in front of the fire Saturdays," he said. "Luxury, I know, but there, we could afford it."

"It is lovely," said Gwen. "We shall bring our things down in the morning."

"And all of it," said Owen, "like our old house, built by Tudor hands; all our own work. If they don't like it in Birmingham, well, they need not come to see."

"It's you that will go to sea," said Grandpa Morgan Jones. "But you have forgotten something, Tudor."

"You have forgotten to go home, Morgan Jones," said Owen. "But you have been a big help."

"When I was young there were stories," said Grandpa Morgan Jones.

"I think I have heard you tell them all," said Owen. "Many times. So if it is any more, perhaps another time will be better."

"Just a few words," said Grandpa. "Step aside please, Owen Tudor, and listen. Before any of your people came to the valley there were people living here."

"The fairies," said Owen. "I know that."

"In this very pond", said Grandpa Morgan Jones, "there is an Afanc, a monster. Long ago they tried to drag it out with oxen, but, you see, it was no use, and the creature is in here still."

"Well, that is nonsense," said Owen, hoping very much that it was so.

41

"Well, think," said Grandpa. "How is it that no one has ever wanted to own this pond?"

"It is true, no one does," said Owen.

"No one wants to own an Afanc," said Grandpa. "So what are you going to do?"

"Say nothing," said Owen. "I am here now. You should have spoken before."

"Well, it is a very old tale," said Grandpa. "And you have only just done this dangerous thing. But when you are going down its throat remember I did my best. Good night, Tudor."

"Good night, Mr Morgan Jones," said Owen. And Gwen asked what Grandpa had wanted.

"Just rambling on," said Owen. "Just old tales, got no idea of the proper time or place."

SIX

ALL AT ONCE, after a few goodbyes, and hoping we shall see you, Gwen, and, Oh, my dear Mrs Morgan Jones, and Grandpa Morgan Jones muttering through a muddy tangle hanging from his chin about tears only adding to the flood, salt water is bad for dams; all at once the valley was completely empty of everyone but the Tudor family. Only the man from the Council went without a goodbye to Owen and family, or even to the building he wished to say goodbye to. He had what he wanted, and did not even say "Thank you".

"Just the four of us, standing here in the dark," said Myfanwy. The last plodgy footstep had stopped and everybody was gone.

"Well," said Owen, "that's how it is, girl."

"Don't be fanciful, Muff," said Gwen. "You got to count in the cows, living in the next room."

"And Angharad and Delyth," said David.

At the top of the new road, where it went across the dam, a little car-light flickered red, and was gone. Grandpa Morgan Jones had shut the new gate that was there, and from now on only the water company could walk on the land.

"All the same," said Owen, "tomorrow we get our

furniture down and move in. The land has been stolen now, but at least no one else will ever walk on it."

He sat by his fire that night for the last time, dreaming ancient legends of lands lost under the sea.

All the same, thought Gwen, thinking a different sameness, it would be pleasant to have new neighbours, just to exchange a few words now and then.

She had no time to think of such things for the rest of the week. It took more than one day to move house. And Owen had other things to do, as well, like moving the kitchen range and putting it into the Ark.

"Just when the weather is getting cold we are without a fire for three nights," said Gwen. "I am not grumbling, but you better have the right answer, Owen."

"I shall go to bed early," said Owen. But on the Ark going to bed sooner left you longer for being woken by the cows shouting in the night. Or for hearing the sheep jumping over gates in their part of the vessel. Or for listening to the long and thumpy conversations of Angharad and Delyth. And Marged the donkey went off like a mad cuckoo clock at all hours of the night, waking the cockerel, who cranked himself up to a metallic sneeze long before first light.

"And", said Gwen, after her first night on board, "there is something scratching in the wall. It is a rat, Owen."

"Then we aren't sinking yet," said Owen. "Rats are the first to know."

"A little eye looking at me through a knot-hole," said Myfanwy. "Mice."

44

All the cats sat about in the empty farmhouse, waiting for their people to return.

Still the Ark was sitting on the bottom of a pond. Owen could see water all round, but it still had to be a wet day. And the river, though the dam blocked its way, seemed to spread in quite the other direction and get higher over there, not over here.

One day Gwen was just pouring a cup of tea when the cup got up and walked across the table, complete with its saucer. The clever tea tried to follow it, but ended up splashed across the cloth. The cup got to the edge of the table, had a look at the floor, rattled its teaspoon, and came back to Gwen.

Gwen had by now put down the teapot, clutched at the wall, and gone outside into the rain.

"There now, marvellous," Owen was saying. "About time too."

"Do you know that the building is falling down?" said Gwen. She said it loudly, somewhere between angry and frightened.

"No, no," said Owen. "The water has come to us at last and lifted us from the bottom of the pond."

"It was like a cow getting up," said Gwen. "Lumpy and bumpy."

"The water has filled up the other side of the valley, and now it's our turn," said Owen. "See, look, the wind making it lift up and down coming along in quite a wave."

But he was thinking just then of an Afanc getting up like a cow, bumpy and lumpy, after being asleep since the time of the fairies. But Grandpa Morgan Jones could never be right, because all his stories were legends, even the ones about himself.

Gwen looked out across the valley, but it was

tea-time and getting dark, and all she saw was grey water and grey sky, and a few black specks.

"Birds," she said. "Lost their nests, they have."

"Goronwy's buildings are going under water," said Owen. "That's where they were. But we are floating at last. I shall check the anchor."

Don't want Afanc biting through it, he thought. But he kept the worry to himself.

Gwen thought she would not go inside again, ever, with the floor moving, the cups travelling, the tea spouting where it liked. But she was driven indoors whether she liked it or not, because the black specks were not birds but bats, who all came to live in the roof of the Ark.

"I should have blocked up the holes," said Owen. "Well, there's room."

"I hope so," said Gwen. "Another room entirely," because she did not want things entangled in her hair.

Owen anchored the Ark to the willow tree at the edge of the pond, where it hung over the water. "Anywhere above the pond is free for us," he said.

For a few more days it was possible to leave the Ark. But one night the ramp lifted itself up when the end of the Ark did. When Owen went down the next morning he stepped off the end as usual. He expected water nearly as deep as his gumboot, but not actually inside the boot. Or really above his knee. As for having it tightly round his waist, cold and clinging, that was very unexpected. Also, the Ark and the ramp separated, so Owen was shipwrecked quite early in the voyage.

He was able to walk on to the land, but the land was no longer home. He shouted, and he shouted, but he was on the starboard side of the Ark and the rest of the family slept on the port side. What was more, the port side had no land at all, only water right to the far side of the valley, so Owen could not get round there at all.

It was ten past six in the morning. Owen stamped through the muds and waters of the old road as far as Mrs Morgan Jones's house and climbed through a window. But there was neither bed nor breakfast to be had there. There was not even an old abandoned kettle. He made a fire and burnt an old chair, a box that said Bacon and Cig Moch, which is the Welsh for it, and breakfasted on the smell, bedding on the bare floor.

A long time later, when he was getting nicely dry, a car came down the flooding street as far as it dared.

"No sin in taking shelter, I hope," thought Owen, when he heard someone trying the door. "Just coming," he shouted.

"Just a tramp," said a man at the door to another one.

"Indeed," said Owen. "Where? And don't I know you? It was you came and measured my fields, and don't know between a cow and bullock, isn't it?"

"We saw some smoke," said the man. He was one of those from the black van, and the same van was behind him now. "We own the land, does Birmingham, and people must stay away."

Owen looked away along the street and beyond. He could see the Ark, and that smoke was coming from its chimney.

"I'll be off home, then," he said.

"It would be better," said the man. "We can make you stay away."

"Well, I won't argue," said Owen. But he said later to Gwen what he was thinking, that they could make him stay off the land, but not make him stay away, because he was in the middle of it; or the pond was.

He paddled back nearer to the Ark, and called until David threw him a rope. Then he pulled himself through the water, climbed the side, and was aboard again.

"Never touched the cows yet," he said. "You see to them David. I think I've got an argument coming on."

He had an argument coming on. The two men followed him to the edge of the water and saw where he went.

"Can't believe their eyes," Owen said to Gwen. "We've outwitted them."

"I don't call getting soaked to the skin outwitting anyone," said Gwen. "Outwetting, more like. Now they're shouting to you."

There was a bit of a shout, about not trespassing on our land, it belongs to Birmingham, and we'll have the law on you, and we'll have to report this, and you can't get away with it.

"You'll see," said Owen. But he was not shouting. The men had to come close to hear him, and to do that they came knee-deep in cold water.

"Their best trousers," said Gwen. "Good shoes."

"That's the sort they are," said Owen. "Tourists."

"But it's an act of parliament," the men were saying.

"Over in England they can act what they like," said Owen. "But this is Wales, and not even the land of Wales but its pond. I'm allowed on this pond, and that's where I'll stay."

48

Well, the men argued, and they were cross; they pleaded and were nice; they stood until they shivered.

"You'd better come up and have a cup of tea," said Gwen, at last. "No law against that, eh?"

"Very likely," said the men. "But kindly of you, if we may."

"Owen will haul you up," said Gwen. "You can talk in the kitchen." Then, being Gwen, the cup of tea brought its friends along, so there was porridge, and bacon, or cig moch, and eggs, or wyau, while Owen said unkind things about the English, or Saeson, and the men did not say unkind things about him or Gwen while she gave them her own bread, and butter, and jam and cream.

"But, you cannot do it," they said. "We are bound to get the law on you."

"How?" said Owen. "A submarine?"

"We shall think of something," said the men.

"Well, I had better be prepared," said Owen. "There is something I have overlooked. Post a letter for me in the town, will you be so kind? I shall write it and put it in the envelope, and you have some more bread from the oven."

He sat on his bed and wrote a short letter. He sealed it in an envelope, wrote the address on the outside, and stuck a stamp on it.

"It is Royal Mail now," he said. "You cannot open it. It has a Welsh stamp on it, and the Queen's picture. And, notice, she is part Tudor herself, so look out you take care of it."

"You can trust us," said the men. Owen felt he could trust them as men, but not when they were Birmingham.

They went. They got their feet and their trousers wet again, but that could not be helped. Their van had filled with water, and they were not happy with that.

"Keep it dry," said Owen, meaning his letter. So everybody waved, and it was friendly in the end.

"You are trusting with the letter," said Gwen. "They will know your plans, reading it somehow. Someone will know Welsh, whatever you write."

"Do not worry," said Owen. "It is the thing I forgot about, quite and entirely. What I have sent for to Swansea, is a little rowing boat, so we can get about. It is a thing Noah would have been glad of, and so shall we be too."

"Mrs Noah would have liked it too," said Gwen.

SEVEN

THE WATER WENT on rising. From now on the Ark was never quite still, because the wind moved it on the water, and the water moved it without any help. But the big shake that had spilt the tea did not happen again. It had been caused by the Ark unsticking itself from the mud at the bottom of the pond and coming loose all at once.

At first the willow tree was alongside, with its hanging branches showing at the bedroom windows. But gradually the branches hung lower and lower, or the Ark rose up beside them, until even Owen could not reach them by hanging out over the side.

"I don't want a handful of twigs with no leaves on," he said. The leaves had all fallen away as the winter came on. "At least we do not have to sweep them off the deck."

The little rowing boat came from Swansea. A huge wagon delivered it to the water's edge, and the box stood on the tailgate.

"Can't get it to the premises," said the driver. "I've only got a little trolley. You got a boat or anything?"

"Yes," said Owen. "Thank you."

But the man did not understand until everything was explained, with the wagon grumbling impatiently behind him and water trickling into its exhaust pipe making a worse noise than Grandpa Morgan Jones's pipe on a rainy day.

"Not a sailor," he said at last, when Owen waded to him. "Just drop it in the water, is that right?"

"That's it," said Owen. "It'll float." Between them they dropped the box from the tailgate. Of course it sank at once, because the boat was not put together, and it is the shape that makes it float, not the stuff it is made from.

"Don't blame me," said the driver. "You're the one that can't be told. They were telling me that when I asked the way. Up the pond, they said, but that is a big pond." He looked out over the spreading waters. "Sign here please, thank you. When I was a boy we had frogspawn and tiddlers and newts. What do you have in this? Whales' eggs, sharks, and dragons?"

"The Afanc, swimming about loose," said Owen. "Got a taste for wagons, if you hang about too long."

"I heard of that," said the driver. "Is this the lake? But I read they pulled the Afanc out, with oxen."

"The oxen broke," said Owen. "Old Afanc crept back in the pond." You have to say something, he thought, but you don't have to believe it.

The man did. "I'm off," he said. The wagon went away. Owen stood on his box and worked out what to do, and then did it. He put the boat together full of water, then bailed it dry, found the oars, got the box itself from the water, put it in the boat, and took it to the Ark.

"I am taking it home," he said to himself. "That is where I live." But at the same time he had a small thought, like a silvery fish in the lake of his mind, that home was a little different in the old days.

He rowed out next morning, without being used to boats at all. He wanted to step on green fields again while there still were some.

"Be careful," said Gwen. "And why are you taking the dogs? They are frightened and rolling their eyes."

"Taking them for a walk," said Owen. "Come back, Bess, come back, Lyart."

The dogs would go anywhere with him, he knew, but not in a boat. They preferred to swim alongside.

"They are frightened of falling in," said Myfanwy.

The dogs had a big run on land, in and out of fields. There were no gates now, and they could go anywhere.

Owen went up to the house, and the dogs thought they should settle in their old place there, on the straw and the black stones.

"Our time here is over," said Owen, looking in through his windows at the empty rooms. The damp and cold had made the wallpaper curl from the walls, and a drip of water from a cracked slate had wet the floor. And the dogs said that a fox was living in the dairy.

But from the chimney end of the house the white doves came down in hope of being fed, and stood round Owen's feet while he pulled the last of the cabbages and the best of the parsnips from the garden.

When he had done that he turned to go indoors again, to find the door locked, the family no longer there, his own house not his any more.

So he looked out, wanting to sneeze with feeling he did not understand, and saw the Ark floating on the waters.

"I am homesick," he said. "I am homesick for all

my ancestors who ever lived here before me, and for all who should live here after me. But what do they know of that in Birmingham? They never had ancestors worth a button. And no matter how sad I feel, I shall not be beaten by them."

He packed a basket full from the garden, and took it back to the Ark.

"Thank you," said Gwen. "Ready washed, I see."

"It seemed simplest," said Owen. "There I was in the biggest sink in the land, so I just dipped them in and swilled them about."

"Visiting the old house has made you unhappy," said Gwen.

"I don't know," said Owen. "I was happy before, all those years, but it's hard to tell at the time just how much it was."

Then Myfanwy came running into the kitchen with a handful of kittens, their eyes just open and looking about. She had found a nest made by one of the five cats, which had at last followed them down.

"Back in the hay," she said. "Stripy ones, orangey ones, black and white, seven of them, and the mother is the tabby with a white tip to her tail. She doesn't mind if I play with them."

"All the same," said Gwen, "our cats are yard cats, so don't bring them in the kitchen. She will want them back now."

"And no neighbours to give them to," said Owen. "Well, what's a few kittens extra? There's plenty of room, and the more hay the cows eat the more room there'll be, and so much milk when the cows calve. They'll be next, I dare say."

He changed his mind when he visited the pigs. The

oldest sow, with the best sty right at the front of the Ark, was going to be next.

"There'll be some piglets any day," he said. "She always has a good litter, and it won't be long now."

Gwen was waking in the night and hearing squeaks and squeals. She was sympathetic about young creatures, but was certain that what she could hear was a nest of rats, just behind her bed.

"Don't worry," said Owen. "We have plenty of cats coming along, seven new ones just learning to hunt, following their mother about."

Myfanwy found it sad that a day or two later there were only six of the litter left. David saw what had happened. The kittens had followed their mother about the Ark, but the middle one, who was always getting into trouble anyway, and was not good at jumping, had lost his footing and dropped down into the water. Owen had been away in the boat, and though Myfanwy threw down firewood and straw and rope-ends, the kitten had drifted away, and was never heard of again.

"Nothing came up to eat it?" said Owen, when he returned. He was thinking of Afancs.

"Nothing. Just eleven cats left," said Myfanwy. "That's poverty."

Later on David came in. He had been looking for a new sack of pigmeal, and found another litter of eight kittens. "Blind as bats still," he said.

"Not bats too," said Gwen.

And Owen came hurrying to the kitchen. "She's started," he said. "One little boar so far, and plenty more to come."

At the bows of the Ark the eldest sow lay apparently asleep, with a smile on her face. At the other end of her, one by one, knowing exactly what to do, pink and speckly piglets were being born like little clockwork things, sniffing the air, and going round the corner for a suck of milk.

"Beautiful," said Owen. "There's farming, boyo, proper." He stroked a piglet's nose and it squealed happily. At any rate, the other end of the sow stayed asleep.

EIGHT

ONE DAY THE willow tree was no longer there. Gwen thought it had been washed away, because trees do not vanish to nothing quite so completely. "Or the anchor has broken, Owen."

"We're still here," said Owen. "The tree is still there, but down under the water." He pulled at the anchor rope, and it was still fastened firmly. "We are in the same place," he said. "Look one way and the chimneys of the Swyddfa'r Post and Mrs Morgan Jones's house are all lined up; and look the other way and our old house is just lined up against the wood. Look, see, there's our doves taking a flight out and sitting on the roof."

So they were, a little fountain of birds, walking about on the blue slates.

"I could just hear them," said Gwen. "And I'd be thinking, stay away and don't mess my washing. But look, Owen, how the water's getting up the track."

The water was creeping higher up the hillside. Owen would look at it and think of the drowned fields; Gwen would remember that mushrooms grew best there, where Angharad and Delyth grazed; David thought about the apple trees in the hedge; and Myfanwy still expected, somehow, to see Postman

Griffith bicycle up out of the water, dry as a letter, and deliver the mail.

The rising water did not only come up the sides of the valley. Here and there beside the river there were little hills. The little hills gradually became islands, and on those islands were wild animals that were not happy about swimming, and who did not have enough to eat.

"We shall do something about it," said Myfanwy. "Birmingham does not care, but I do. I shall take the boat and rescue them."

"Of course," said Owen. "After all, you are not going to school, so you have nothing to do."

Myfanwy thought she had plenty to do, with piglets and kittens, and a lot of worrying about how to be fair to rats. "David will help too," she said.

David rowed her out to one little hilltop after another, trying to clear them one by one. They took hay with them for those they could not manage that day.

"They kick and they scratch and they bite," said Myfanwy that night. "Some are rabbits, some are hares, which are very cross, and there are stoats and weasels."

"Indeed," said Gwen. "Go and wash your hands."

"Hedgehogs," said David. "You get prickled too. And there were snakes."

"Poison bites, those," said Gwen. "Farming is one thing, but vermin is another. Still, can't leave them to drown. And they got nothing for losing their homes, so I am sorry for them."

"We've got somewhere to eat and sleep," said Owen. "And now time for you two to be off to bed, now you've had supper."

58

Much later on Owen went out to look at the night before going to bed himself. He took three strides across the deck, and felt it was giving way under him.

"What is it?" asked Gwen, hearing a cracking and crunching noise with each stride.

"Bring a lantern," said Owen. "I do not know. There is something on the deck."

There were seven saucers on the deck, and Owen had trodden on them all. There had been milk in them, and that made a large puddle.

"Myfanwy has been feeding the kittens," said Owen. "We shall have to tell her to do it somewhere else." He pitched the broken saucers overboard and swilled the milk away.

Gwen went in again and began to pull on her slippers, which had been kept warm in the cupboard beside the fire.

But the slippers curled up and were sharp all over, and there was a shriek from Gwen. Owen came hurrying in, saw what was going on, and understood what the saucers had been for.

He woke Myfanwy and made her take away seven hedgehogs, curled up round the living accommodation. There were also some blinky rabbits under her bed. And David knew about a pair of stoats that had gone to ground under the hay. The snake, he said, was asleep in a box.

"Out," said Gwen. "All of them out in the morning."

"But it is a rescue," said Myfanwy. "And this is an Ark."

"There is a lot of Wales left," said Gwen. "It is taking our bit we are complaining of. And I am not complaining about animals. It's not as if they spoke

English or anything bad. But they will be happier in the wild."

Goronwy's last barn by the river had its roof made into an island, and its owl left her home. She perched on the Ark for a night or two, a too-whit or two, and then flew away.

"Pity," said Owen. "I was thinking of making her a nesting hole up under the eaves. Owls are friendly and good luck."

One day Lyart, the brindled dog, stood in the bows of the Ark and barked at something ashore. There were men with a tractor coming to the village, to the Swyddfa'r Post, to Mrs Morgan Jones's bed and breakfast, to Grandpa Morgan Jones's cottage, climbing on the roofs.

"Just come for the view," said Owen. "I hope we are not getting in the news or anything ridiculous. Only laugh at us, they will. Is it cameras they have?"

"Hammers," said David. "They are doing something, but on the far side, so I cannot see."

"We shall stay out of the way," said Owen. "But keep an eye."

Hammering went on in the village. The tractor, its trailer, and more men, went across the fields, breaking hedges, not caring at all, until they came to the farmhouse.

"Do not get angry," said Gwen, because Owen was walking up and down, shaking with feeling.

"It is not ours," said Owen. "I know. But I do not like them to come near, indeed I do not."

"I will make some tea," said Gwen. "You are not to become upset."

"Tourists," said Owen. "I cannot abide tourists."

When he saw what was happening, though, he

thought there was sense in it. "But I cannot imagine anything more sad," he said. "What else could they do to break a man's heart? What is there more cruel?"

The men with the tractor were not tourists. They had come to take the slates from the roofs, to use on another building. "I daresay it is on the building for the dam," said Gwen. "It is in keeping with the style."

"They are right," said Owen. But he looked at the bare wood of the roof, with the hillside showing through the spars, and felt that he had been taken to pieces himself.

"Every one of those slates came from the quarry long before any Grandpa Morgan Jones picked at it," he said. "But dismantled before our very eyes, that is heartless."

Then the men went, the trailer full of slates. "Like poachers," said Gwen.

"Just a builder from town," said Owen. "I know him. I bought the best part of this wood from him. No, just sadness. Perhaps we should have gone away, right or not. I hope I have not brought sorrow on you all."

By next morning he felt better. "A waste to let them rot under water," he said. "I'll take my dinner out in the boat, today, Gwen. David and I will row right across and up and take a look at the old quarry before it goes too. It has been put in my mind, and there is not much else left to see."

It was a long pull to the far side of the valley now, and a longer one to the quarry itself. Behind them, which is what Owen saw as he rowed, the Ark grew smaller and smaller, and the dam itself seemed larger and larger.

Then they were rounding the bend of the valley. "Just here it would be getting steeper if we were walking," said Owen. "The water is flattish on top."

"I have caught a fish," said David. But it was part of a signpost directing travellers to the village.

"We are just at the turn to the quarry," said Owen. "The road goes over into Cwmfach just there. We shall turn to the right. Can you see it ahead?"

The quarry was like a cliff rising from the water. The floor of it was covered, and grass was growing in the road. At the top was green grass and a fence.

"They couldn't dig any further back, because they would be in the next valley at the top of the hill," said Owen. "Used to be a little shed and a boiler. And there, those red things, where the trucks used to run up the rails. To think, Grandpa Morgan Jones dug most of this out himself, by what he says."

They ate their dinners in the boat, and would have been high up the cliff, if it had been dry land, but at water level, since it wasn't. Then they tied up for a little while to one of the rails and walked up the side of the hill and looked over into Cwmfach.

"Nice little place, this valley," said Owen. "Someone's lucky to have the land."

"There he is, putting in a fence post," said David. So they waved at the man driving a stake in, so far away that the noise of his hammer got to them before it hit the wood, but was from the last hit, of course, not the next. When he had finished everybody waved, and Owen rowed home to the Ark again.

Myfanwy was waiting for them. "Guess what," she said. "Bess, our black dog, has had seven puppies."

"There's room for all," said Owen. "Goodness, yes."

NINE

ONE MORNING WINTER happened. All night long the Ark had been creaking to itself, all its wood and nails moving a little bit, its roof making little but long snapping noises as if the moon had been walking up, then down, from one side to the other.

"It's not the rats," said Gwen. "I know their noises. Are we sinking, Owen? Is it shipwreck that sounds like that?"

"It is the cold night," said Owen. "Our old roof would move and groan under the slates in frosty weather."

"There will be ice on the lake," said David. "Skating."

It was Myfanwy who found all that there was, getting up earlier even than Owen to look at puppies, kittens, some eggs a hen was sitting on, and to scratch at the back of piglets and sow.

Her window was looking at her all white, like the drawing of a forest. She breathed a window in the window with her breath, but still could not see out.

She went to see the families, and found her bare feet getting cold, cold, cold. Owen got up, and she heard his boots clumping on the plain wooden floors. She went into the kitchen to set the fire going. It did not want to burn, and pushed smoke into the house.

"Just stay in bed a bit longer, Mum," she said.

"Glad to," said Gwen.

"I'll get some coals," said Myfanwy, stepping out of the door, cold feet or not, because it was only a few paces to the coal bunker, and the light from the kitchen would show the way.

But for some reason the light did not shine very well, and Myfanwy became lost outside her own door. She was all at once in a strange place she could not see, with thick air getting in her throat.

She dropped the coal shovel, then trod on it so that it hit her ankles. She stretched out her hands and there was nothing at her fingertips. And the cold crawled into her sleeves. She called for Mum.

"It's a fog," said Gwen. She had come to the kitchen door, reached out a hand into darkness, and found Myfanwy. "It's as thick as feathers. Da will get us some coal in a minute, but there's enough here to boil a kettle."

When Owen went for coal a magical bit began. By then the fog had turned white and glowing, with the sunshine not far away overhead. The Ark itself, every piece of it above water, was painted thick with frost, all over sparkle, roof, deck, sides, windows. All round it the lake was like glass, as if it would never have a ripple on it again, strong enough to walk on, but not ice at all, making perfect reflections.

"We shall go out in the boat and look at it," said Owen.

From the boat they saw the Ark suddenly light up when the sunshine came through the mist, like a sudden fire. The fog lifted and lifted, until the sky was blue, the water was blue, the hills all round white with frost. And then the frost melted from the Ark and its wood shone yellow.

"Pretty," said Gwen.

"Well, it does look like a slab of butter on a dish," said Owen, thinking of breakfast.

"Come back," barked Lyart from the deck.

That day was to tell them that winter can be like summer. The next day, and many after that, told them that winter can be like winter. It rained for most of every day, so that going out for a breath of air was uncomfortable.

"I wish I could plod across the yard and see to the cows," said Owen. "It would just make a change. Instead of sailing round the world in the same place all the time." But he said it to himself only.

David and Myfanwy had two great quarrels. Myfanwy went to live with the sheep. "They do not make unkind remarks," she said.

"Just a day in the market would be a change, Owen," said Gwen. "Soaked through getting there and back is nothing."

"I don't like to leave," said Owen. "Birmingham might sink the Ark, or come aboard. Pirates, you see."

"Lyart will see them off," said David. "Even Bess will come to defend her pups."

"Lyart is getting dreadful fat," said Myfanwy.

"Nobody is watching us," said Gwen. "We could go and be back in no time. I would just like tea in the tea-shop, and buy some wool. There's knitting to do."

"Well," said Owen, "I was hoping to get away without Christmas shopping this year, but I see I shan't."

"You never have yet," said Gwen.

"And you never will," said Myfanwy. "I knew I was looking forward to something."

Owen borrowed a tractor from a farmer beyond the hill, and they rode down and back in the trailer. They met Mrs Morgan Jones, but not Grandpa.

"He's gone to live with my cousin in a little place where he was a boy," said Mrs Morgan Jones. "I hear they can't stand him either, but I miss him. Now you must all come and see my new bed and breakfast I started up in town."

"I'm off to look at cows," said Owen.

"And me to sheep," said David.

"And we have urgent business in the shops, Mrs Morgan Jones, but thank you kindly and I do mean it," said Gwen.

There were four boatloads to bring across in the dark when they were home again. When Owen came in at last the day was well over, and the cows were calling for attention.

After all the rain, Christmas Day brought a strange feeling to them. The rain had raised the level of the lake so much that on that very morning Owen looked back towards the old farmhouse, and he could not see it. Only the chimney just showed itself, and that could not be seen because bewildered white doves were fluttering round it, their homes flooded, their feeding places covered in water.

Owen had planned to go that very morning to the little wood behind the house and bring back a Christmas Tree, to stand on deck and be hung with baubles before anyone else came out.

Santa Claus had been, quietly in the night without waking Bess or the stout Lyart, and David and

Myfanwy were discussing gifts with Gwen, who was sitting up in bed drinking a cup of tea and knitting. So no one would see Owen or his journey.

He took a pocketful of grain with him, because he could not let the birds starve. He brought the Christmas Tree, just as he intended, but it was already decorated with white doves. They cooed to him as he rowed across the water.

At the Ark they stood on the roof and waited patiently for Owen to build them somewhere to live.

"My day off work for the year," he said, "and I have to do this for them. See them watching! I've been married long enough to know when I am being ordered about without a word."

He built them pigeon holes under the eaves, and they inspected them and moved in. It took his mind away from being without even the sight of his old home.

The Tudor family had a small pig for their dinner.

"You will eat it, I hope, Muff," said Gwen.

"She has not missed it," said Myfanwy. "She would eat it herself if it got squashed."

By the end of Christmas Day, after the last little ribs of cold piglet for supper, Owen felt clearly that their old life was over.

"What we are doing is not strange any more," he said. "We just live here, over the old pond, that's all. They daren't say a word in Birmingham. I wouldn't be surprised if you didn't get to school again, you two."

"It would be nice to see my friends again," said Myfanwy.

"And I haven't had a good fight in a long time," said David. "Friendly, you know."

"I have," said Owen. "We've beaten Birmingham."

On the last day of the year Birmingham came back with the next part of their fight. They didn't feel beaten.

The two men came to the side of the dam one afternoon, when snow was lying on the land, and the lake itself was growing sudden scales of ice that melted at once. An inflatable boat was pumped up hard, a little engine started, and the boat came bright yellow and smart black across the water.

"Hit an iceberg, they will," said Owen. "Come to admit defeat, that's what."

"They wouldn't have the manners," said Gwen.

"Maybe not coming here at all then," said Owen.

And, after all, the boat went past, up to the top end of the lake.

"Told you so," said Owen. But he was not going to be quite certain until the inflatable was emptied of air, rolled up, and taken quite away.

The next thing they knew was a wasp-coloured bump against the side of the Ark, and a shout.

"Mr Tudor, is it?" said Owen. "Mr Tudor is me. Well, you come to tell me I'm right, I can stay here? Is that it?"

"That's right," said the first man. "Exactly that. Can we come up."

"I won't rub it in," said Owen. "I won't say I told you so, or anything like that. But I knew I was right, and Gwen shall make you a cup of tea, and David, put Lyart back."

"A cup of tea would be good," said the second man. "Cold work out here on your pond."

"I'm in the right place," said Owen. "I hope I am, but the landmarks got under water in the end.

Anchor rope goes straight down, though, so I think I'm right there too."

"We aren't bothered about a few yards either way," said the first man. "Isn't that so?"

"Yes," said the second. "Got to allow for a bit of float, wind pushing, anchor dragging, that sort of thing. Get it all the time."

"Have to be reasonable," said the first man.

They were in the kitchen now, having their tea, playing with puppies and kittens, eating currant bread and butter.

"You'll be ready for anything here, then?" said the second man. "Self-sufficient, eh?"

"Oh, nicely, thank you," said Owen. "Fact is, though, getting a bit overstocked. But pigs coming along nicely for market, and calves due, and puppies nearly ready."

"Market, eh?" said the first man. "I think we've finished our cup of tea, and thank you kindly, Mr and Mrs Tudor. So that's settled then, we agree you can stay on the old village pond, no difficulty there. We forgot to make arrangements to buy it."

"Silly us," said the second man. "Little mistake, and clever of you to find it out. We asked a judge about the law, and he told us."

"But all the same," said the first man, "we've got to give you this paper from the judge too. You'd better look at it carefully, Mr Tudor, because there isn't a little mistake about that. You can stay on the pond as long as you like. But if you set foot ashore, why, the policeman will come for you, and it's the lock-up for you."

The waspy engine started up and the rubber boat sped away. No one looked back.

"Well," said Owen. "I am looking a fool. We shall just have to stay where we are. It is what I meant, but not how I meant it."

"Owen," said Gwen. "They have won. But we are on your side, and we shall stay here with you."

"It's here or the lock-up," said Owen. "I choose here." But he could see there would be difficulties. "I'm too proud to leave," he said. "And if I do, it's against the law."

"I'm not going in the lock-up without a kitten," said Myfanwy. "And they can't do cruelty to animals."

TEN

THE NEXT DAY was the most dismal anyone could remember. The weather was bleak and shrieky, with a cold little wind flinging a hard haily sleet into everyone's face if they looked out of the door. No cat would venture out, and when Lyart took her tubby self for a walk it was with her tail between her legs, most unhappy.

Owen himself would have made a world unhappy too. It was best not to speak to him, Myfanwy found. Gwen did a huge baking, pies, puddings, bread, cake, custard. But the fire seemed to burn cold, and everything came from the oven or steamer flat and sad, sprinkled with soot.

"Well, I could not eat it if the plates was gold," said Owen. Lyart put her head on his knee. "Go on away out of the kitchen, you," said Owen.

Lyart crawled out. The cold weather was kinder, she thought. Gwen looked at Owen. She said nothing, but Owen got up and went for a walk round the deck himself. Gwen took his big chair and sat in it herself.

"It's not often I take the weight from my feet," she said. "But today is one of those days, nothing gone right. My goodness, look at the pair of them, that dog with its tail tucked in, and your Da much the same."

"We're staying," said Myfanwy. "We've got our friends."

"I'm sure we are," said Gwen. "There's stubborn. And there's Owen. Nothing to choose between them, except that Owen is worse by far."

In the end David took a huge mug of tea to Owen. "Man's work," he told his mother.

"Send the poor dog in," said Myfanwy.

David crunched across the snowy deck, a mug in each hand.

"Well, ta," said Owen, taking his in both hands and stamping his feet. David stood beside him and they looked out over the rail, their backs to the wind.

"There's no good way round to be," said Owen. "Makes a good mug of tea, your Ma."

"The steam thaws your face," said David.

"It's my heart and soul I worry about," said Owen. "What can we do? We can't even tell anyone. The lake is getting bigger, but the pond is getting smaller."

So they leaned there and sipped tea, and the dusk fell round them with the sleet.

"Should be going round the houses today," said Owen. "First of the year, crossing the thresholds. Some old New Year it's going to be. They will be forgetting us all if we do not visit."

David dripped his tea-leaves into the water, but it was too dark to see his fortune. The mug turned cold now it was empty.

"Send messages with the doves," he said.

Owen rumpled his hair for him. "Wish it would work," he said. "Rude message to that old judge, first off. No, boyo, come and see to the cows with me. We got all that to do. There won't be anything else happening today."

They finished the cows and felt a little more comfortable.

Then they had a word with Angharad and Delyth. "Hey ho, my beauties," said Owen, and they blew their warm dry breath over him.

Then there were the pigs. The little ones were stamping about manfully, and one of the other sows was looking extremely thoughtful.

"We won't count them before they hatch," said Owen.

They visited the hens. Seven of them had nothing to do but sit on eggs, and the other seven actually did the work of laying them.

Five geese lived in the stern of the Ark, in their dirty nests. They hissed and gabbled. "Thinking it's Christmas," said Owen. "We had a piglet, you silly girls."

The sheep loved to see them, and came forward to have their noses rubbed; or they put up with it to get a few sheep nuts.

"You'd think they were bred to life on the water," said Owen. "But there's nowhere else for them to go except the lock-up."

The little old donkey, Marged, was so pleased to see them she went on singing for an hour afterwards, as if the Ark had a noisy and leaky engine, or some sort of foghorn.

Lyart had gone into the coalhole in the end, because no one wanted her. Owen went for coal and dug up a shovel of puppies. She had seven salt-and-pepper ones just like herself, and came into the kitchen as slim as a comb for a bit of something to eat.

"You'll be feeling better," said Gwen, giving her some failed pudding. "Seven, is it? And they say dogs can't count."

By the time Myfanwy had carried the puppies down to a better place in one of the hay stores, and Lyart had gone back and forth checking the numbers, then forgetting the answer and going back and forth again, it was quite dark outside, and very cold.

"Just think," said Owen, taking a last turn round the deck. "There isn't another light to be seen. We are all alone. If the world ended out there we would never know, and we daren't go to find out."

So the day was ending as hopelessly as it began. Gwen could not speak. She expected all days from now on to be without hope too. She cleared her throat.

"I know how you feel," said Owen. "It was never like this for Noah, people going to law on him."

"If there was a star I would wish on it," said Gwen.

"On a bad old night like this," said Owen.

But the cloud overhead did thin a little, and somehow the sky seemed clearer in one place.

"It's just twinkle in my eyes," said Gwen. "It would be cheating to wish on that . . . Owen, Owen, look, look at that . . ."

Owen looked. Gwen looked. Myfanwy laughed, the first time anyone had done such a thing that day, that year. David gave a howl of delight.

Out of the clear patch of sky came a star of all stars, flying, seeming to shower sparks, running across space, like a bright message of hope, then fading to nothing, wasted away giving the message.

74

"Shooting star," said Owen. "You got a good wish on that, Gwen, sure to."

"Oh," said Gwen. "I forgot, it was so sudden. But it was too good to wish on. That was our luck just as it is, Owen. We are to be lucky after all."

"I wish I knew how," said Owen. "But it is true, isn't it?"

"There's no one else left to tell us anything," said Gwen.

After that there was a winter of snow coming and going, of sharp frosts, of days of sunshine, days of cloud. There were days when the decks had to be cleared of snow before anyone could move. David would sweep and shovel the lumps over the side, where they would turn grey and sink. Once there was a little crust of ice all round, but the wind licked it all away like flakes of torn newspaper.

There was one frosty night that made the timbers groan again, and the cold struck through into all the rooms so that Gwen's breath hung about her in the kitchen even when the fire was roaring.

During it there came a noise that had not been heard before, of some distant thing breaking and falling, like an avalanche, and a little time after it another sound just the same, with the splashing of water following.

Owen listened. He did not know what it was. Then he heard something crossing the water towards the Ark, and by the light of a lantern saw a wave running towards him. He did not have to be a sailor to know that when it hit all along the side of the Ark everyone would be thrown about.

"Hold tight," he called. But since everyone called

75

out, one after another, "What did you say?" no one got the message.

The wave did more than slap the Ark. It rolled it over on its side so the kettle slid across the fire, the sheep lying down rolled on their backs, the hens fell off their clutches of eggs, and Myfanwy rolled out of her bed, out of the door, and under David's bed.

Gwen was in the big chair and quite safe. But the Ark went on rocking, because the wave came back from the shore and walloped the other side. Then there was a second wave, and a second echo from the shore.

By now everyone was clinging on. "It was to do with those noises," said Owen. "The noise comes soon, the wave takes longer."

"Earthquake," said Gwen, fixed in the chair, not minding. "We shall be all right, Owen. We saw the shooting star."

"I am just thinking what it might be," said Owen. "I think the dam has broken, that's what, broken down the middle, all the water running out, and serve them right. They will give it up, they will take it away, and we shall get our land back. Yes, we shall get a new roof, and be back home."

"We shall get washed down into Birmingham, if that is where the water goes," said Gwen. "I shall spend the night in the chair. I cannot fall out."

Owen went to check his anchor rope. It was tight and firm.

"We shall stay here," he said. "Down on the pond in the morning, you see."

But in the morning nothing had changed. The water was at the same level, and calm again, the dam was complete, and Gwen needed a haul to get her from the chair.

"Well, next time," said Owen. "The concrete has cracked, for sure."

He rowed out and had a look at the dam. It looked as if it had just come out of the mould, still perfect, not even covered with moss yet. But Owen knew something had happened, and went, on fine days, to look at other places.

One day he came back fairly sure he had found the cause of the noise. "The old slate quarry," he said. "The weather gets in the rock and breaks it off, and some pieces fell down in the water. There was a great big new place where it had come away, I don't know how many tons. That will be it, for sure."

However, he was not quite so sure of things these days, because they had a way of turning round and giving the wrong answer. "Daren't step ashore," he said, "with rocks falling about, and all that about the lock-up, the policeman lying in wait. Got to get back to milk."

Spring time began to come. It came on the land, with the hills turning green. It came in the sky, with warmer winds. It came in the lake with frogs jumping at the edge and fish at the middle. It came on the trees, with new leaves sprouting.

It came on the Ark as well. Night after night among the sheep there were new small voices shouting, and lambs tried to walk on the moving floor of their hold.

Morning after morning among the cows calves were being born. There were seven little broods of chicks pecking and cheeping round the decks. There were goslings falling on their chins. There were thirty-three more piglets.

There was an exciting time for the little donkey, Marged, because she found a brown and hairy bundle by her feet one afternoon, and did not understand what it was. And the foal was not sure which was its mother, Marged or Myfanwy.

Angharad and Delyth, on the same day, had a foal each, and said quite plainly that they wanted to be out and run in the fields.

Myfanwy sitting desperately on her bed surrounded by puppies and piglets and some young rabbits whose mother she had tamed and very secretly hidden, tried to give all the new young animals names. But there were problems with not having enough names, and an equal problem knowing which of nineteen lambs was called which of nineteen names; and worse with thirty-three identical piglets whose mothers did not know which was whose.

And suddenly they all realised that the rats were shouting for something to be done, for the same reason that Owen was becoming worried and tired.

There were so many living things on board that they could not all stand up at once, and they could not all sit down at once; and it was becoming impossible to walk without treading on someone.

"Well, that's it," said Owen. "No better spring crop has a farmer ever had. But we are running short of hay, and all the animals need grass now. I think I shall have to give myself up, and hope the judge will listen first. I have been so foolish."

But before anyone could talk him out of it there were other more urgent things. The water of the lake began to be rough, and the wind came jumping across it in great puffs and huffs, swinging the Ark about, making the waves higher than they had ever been, so that water splashed in through the kitchen door.

"Storm coming," said Owen. "Close everything up. I will just check the anchor rope."

Before he could do so, before he got to it, he heard it part. He felt the wind take the Ark and blow it where it wanted, twirling and swirling it, dipping and bobbing it.

"Sit in the chair, my love," he shouted to Gwen. "You will be safe there."

"I shall go to bed," said Gwen. "I am not feeling quite my usual self. Perhaps it is the sea sickness."

"I will just move that poorly calf out of the room," said Owen.

"Thank you," said Gwen, and curled up on her bed.

And the Ark, with no sails, no rudder, no more idea of where to go than a cloud, moved on the surface of the waters.

ELEVEN

OWEN WENT OUT on to the deck. The Ark hiccuped under him and he sat down. Luckily it was only in a wet patch, not on any animals. In a corner by the coalhole there was a drift of yellow leaves, packed tight and fluttering a bit as if the edges were torn. Owen got himself up on his knees and picked the leaves up. He opened the kitchen door and dropped them inside, because they were not leaves but little chicks, lost out here in the storm. They scuttled to the fender. Somewhere in the Ark their mother hen called for them, telling them not to go near the water.

"She doesn't know," thought Owen. He found his way to the anchor rope. It was stretched out tight, just as it should be; but it was not tight enough, and he could pull it towards himself, heavy at first, then lighter and lighter, and at last a ragged end, and after that nothing.

The Ark was turning in the wind, and swaying. Owen felt his boots getting heavier and lighter as the deck went up and down, and himself getting lighter and heavier, but never normal. He had been in a lift in Swansea once, going up, but had walked down to keep his head clear.

A wave came up and licked him in the face and all

down his front. Owen decided he was the wrong side of the Ark, and tried the other. The wave had the same thought and gave him another lick from there.

The Ark ran into the top of a tree. There were green leaves on the tree, which had not been altogether drowned. A bough scraped along the side, and Owen put the rope end round it as it looked over the rail.

"That's it," he thought. "The remedy came with the ill, like docks and nettles growing together. This tree will hold us."

He took a few turns more round the branches, and was sure that Ark and tree were tied together for as long as he wanted them to be.

The Ark still rolled and wallowed, but he decided that was with the waves, and with the wind pushing all along one side. He made his way back to the kitchen.

Inside, by the light of the hanging lamp, Myfanwy was picking up the remains of a teapot.

"I was going to make some tea," she said. "But then I did not feel like it."

"No need to be cruel to the pot, girl," said Owen, rubbing his face dry, and feeling the comfortable warmth of the room.

"It jumped off the table," said Myfanwy. "Da, I think I will lie down. The room is going round and round and I feel hot and cold and I am not well. I would rather be in the lock-up, please."

David was already in his room. He knew he was ill. Owen looked in at Gwen.

"Leave me be," she said. "No one is to come in."

"We are tied up to another tree," said Owen, closing the door again.

"I wish it was on dry land," said Myfanwy.

"I am homesick for the land," said Owen. "Yes."

"I am seasick," said Myfanwy, which was dreadful for her. But in a while she fell asleep.

Owen made himself some tea in another pot, and drank it carefully. It slopped about inside him like another storm. He went outside again, because the room was swaying about too much for him too.

The rope was still firmly tied. He felt it with his hands, because everything was now quite dark. There was nothing to be seen anywhere, and only his head and his feet and a sagging feeling in his stomach told him he was going up and down. Just once or twice he thought he saw a distant light, flickering and then vanishing.

The Ark lurched, without any warning. He thought it was diving to the bottom of the lake. Then something hit it extremely hard down under the water, and he was sure it must be sinking. The wind suddenly steadied up, the Ark steadied up with it, and things became calmer.

They were not calm enough for walking about without holding on, but Owen no longer felt that his head, feet, and stomach were thinking wildly different things. They all thought one thing, that the Ark was settling down in the water and sinking.

"I hope it was a little tree," Owen thought. "Not so far to go. But here we are, blind in the dark." And he thought a bit more. "Stubborn, too. I have been stubborn, and look where it has brought us, and no one will care, Owen Tudor drowned a whole farm, careless like."

Slowly, too slow to tell, the sky grew lighter. All the time the storm whistled overhead and shook the Ark; all the time waves broke over it from the front;

and continually something thudded against the bottom of it, like a great drainpipe rolling in the bottom of a trough, scraping and drumming.

Or perhaps biting with great teeth, which was what an Afanc would do, woken by the storm, coming up hungry, attacking the biggest thing in the water.

Any minute now, thought Owen, it will come up for a look, and I shall have nothing to say to it, or to Gwen, or to the children. I could wish that that Morgan Jones was mistaken, him and his stories, no right to be true, that's what.

For the time being no monster lifted its head from the water. It stayed below, banging at the keel of the Ark.

The light sky began to show Owen where he was. He could not understand at first because here was something he had not thought about. He did not know why he was seeing a view down the valley, just the view he would have had from the Swyddfa'r Post, the road winding down, the fields, the town far in the distance, still grey and without colour, still obscured by a great driving rain.

"I can't be," he thought. "There isn't anywhere to see it from, the dam is too high."

Then David came out on deck with him. "Where are we, Da?" he asked, but Owen could not hear him because something made too much noise.

Myfanwy came out too. She understood where they were. She had been here before with Gwen.

"We are on top of the dam," she shouted, and her voice broke through the noise. "We are on top of the waterfall and we shall go down the other side."

It was true. The lake had filled to the top, and the

83

dam could not be seen, because water was spilling and rushing over it. And it was plain what else had happened. The tree Owen had tied up to had come out of the ground and floated up under the Ark, and the flow of the water was taking it to the edge of the dam. The rain falling on them was spray lifted by the wind; the noise was the cataract itself. And the Afanc was not there at all, outside the fancy of Grandpa Morgan Jones.

Owen took out his knife at once. There was only one thing to do, and he did not know whether it would help. He cut the rope that tied them to the tree.

The tree, being nearly all under water, was taken by the water. The Ark, being nearly all out of the water, was taken by the wind. The departing tree gave a serious battering to the bottom of the Ark, then showed dark in the muddy water, and sat itself on the edge of the dam. Then it seemed to climb up, like some great animal, perhaps the Afanc itself, balance at the edge, wave a few goodbyes with its boughs, and disappear.

"It's gone," shouted Owen. "I knew it was just a tale."

Only the boiling rim of water showed now. But it was getting further away. The Ark was being taken by the wind. Owen, Myfanwy, and David felt so much relief at not going over that the pitching and heaving that started again had little effect on them.

They came out of the falling spray and gradually up into the middle of the lake, where there was a strong but dry wind, making some waves slop up the sides of the Ark, but sending it straight up the valley.

They met another shipwreck. The little rowing boat was floating upside down, going its own way.

"We shall get to land in a field," said Owen. "Right way up, out of sight. But it does not seem likely. And there is nothing we can do."

The wind took them up the valley. A long way behind them now the edge of the dam was a faint line with a sort of smoke above it. On either side the hills were full of water, white streams running down from every place and boiling into the lake.

"Just get round the corner, up to the top end," said Owen. "Stands to reason it gets shallower as the ground gets higher. We shall just run nicely up in a little meadow, walk away dry shod, I shouldn't wonder."

He was wrong again. They were to be terrified again. Where the valley turned its corner the wind did not turn too. The wind went straight on. The Ark went straight on with it.

Straight ahead was the only hard place in the valley, the old slate quarry, with its high cliff mostly dug out by Grandpa Morgan Jones.

But no one remembered who had dug anything. All they saw, quite clearly, was that the Ark was making for the cliff, the shipwreckingest place in the valley.

"Not so high as it was," said Owen. The water had risen, of course.

"But just as steep," said David. "The fence at the top has fallen down."

"We are going to hit the cliff," said Owen. "Myfanwy, go and tell your mother. Tell her to come out, we shall have a go at swimming."

Myfanwy did not come back. "Silly things," said

Owen. "They can swim in their nightie, no good getting dressed smart for shipwreck. Noah didn't, you can be sure."

It was clear that nothing would stop the Ark from hitting the cliff head on. The wind itself blew harder, and the Ark went like a thick arrow, into the bay made by the quarry, towards the high stone wall.

"Gwen," shouted Owen, through the door. "Just making silly noises," he said. "Well, there is no time to do anything now, except hold on tight, David."

They held on tight. Suddenly the cliff was not only ahead of them, but was looming over them as well, though not standing much higher. And then the waves which had been forced into the bay gave a sudden lift and push, and the front of the Ark hit the land very hard indeed.

David knew that he sat down and the coal from the coalhole heaped itself on top of him. Owen was sure he himself had stood firm, holding on, upright all the time.

He never understood how he happened to be sitting peacefully in a bush, out of the wind, the sun shining on him, and everything calm.

Overhead a cloud of white doves whirled in the blue sky, carrying leaves in their beaks.

"Dead," he said. "I'm in the good place." Then he discovered that the bush was a gorse bush. "No, wrong again," he said. "But at least", he was able to say, "I am allowed to get out of it."

He was out and standing up, looking round.

"I am in Cwmfach," he told himself. "I have fallen out of the ambulance."

Then he heard a baby crying, and then stop crying and make happy noises. He saw the baby and its mother sitting on a rug spread on a rock, beside a little road, just a few yards away.

"Excuse me," he said, and the gorse prickles were nipping all over him, "can you please tell me where I am, lady?"

"I do not know," said the lady with the baby. It was Gwen. "You brought us here, Owen Tudor."

Owen sat down in amazement. The gorse bush began its work again. "But where did you get this?" he asked, pointing to the baby.

"Muff," called Gwen, and Myfanwy came up with another baby. "While you were sailing the boat I was busy having this, well, litter, I suppose you call it. You have two more sons, Owen Tudor. We should call them Storm and Tempest, but they will be nicer than that."

"They will be Dwyfan and Dwyfach," said Owen.

"Lovely little men," said Myfanwy.

And, "Well done, Da," said David. "It was clever." He was black with coal, but no one was hurt. "How did you know where to sail?"

"You pick up things as you go along," said Owen. "But this, no, I didn't manage a thing."

The Ark had hit the crumbling cliff near its top. The hill the other side was so steep that the cliff was thin and broke through easily. The Ark had gone straight through on a wave of water, and slid down the hillside before anyone knew what was happening. It had then slithered into a little valley, and come to rest the right way up, all in one piece, in a flat place, leaning on a row of trees.

Every door in it had come open, and there were holes in its sides. Now, gradually, with Gwen and her babies first, the animals of the farm were finding their way out into the fields nearby.

Owen leaned on a post and thought about things. He turned and looked at the post. It seemed to him that he and David had seen this very stake being driven in long ago. It was not part of a fence. It held a notice. FOR SALE, it said, desirable farm, known as Cwmfach, how many acres, a farmhouse, and all buildings and a price.

And here was the owner coming up the cwm.

"Go in the kitchen, David," said Owen, "get my cheque book, settle the matter now. We have the money."

The matter was settled immediately. "Moving in at once," said Owen.

"Remember, I told you all the water is to be fetched," said the owner. "Tired of the trouble, I am, after all these years. Makes it hard to sell, that's all."

"That will be all right," said Gwen. "We'll manage."

"We shall start now," said Owen. "Everything to get in order. Cows to milk, haven't been touched today."

"It's like home," said Gwen, seeing the house. "Solid stone, not floating at all."

"Got a new roof on it," said the owner. "Had the slates from the old farm below the wood in the next valley, you know where the lake is now."

"Hope he fixed the leaky bit by the chimney," said Gwen. "You never managed it, Owen, all the time we were there."

"All this we've been through", said Owen, "was the best way to fix the problem."

"I'll send my uncle up to help with things," said the owner. "He finds time hanging on his hands. Talks a bit, but all right."

"Be glad," said Owen.

88

So they started to move beds and chairs and tables into the farm, and put cows into the right fields, fowls in their house, horses in the stables.

"Walking funny, you are," said the helpful uncle of the owner. "Anyone would think you been at sea a long time. I understand horses, Tudor, I'll do those."

But in a moment he was walking funny too. As usual, the horses trod on his foot and bit his beard, because the uncle was Grandpa Morgan Jones, living near his slate quarry.

"Funny to be glad to see him," said Owen.

"Glad to see anyone, nearly," said Gwen. "Now, have we done that baby, Muff, or is that one next? I'm losing count worse than the old sow."

In Birmingham they think the whole farm sank, Owen says. "We are glad they don't care. One day they will begin to worry."

Postman Griffith came up in a day or two with such a pile of letters, and all the Christmas Cards. "Been waiting for you to come out of the water," he said.

Gwen made him wait longer, now he was here. He was glad to, with months and months of chat to catch up with, and a big shortage of cups of tea.

Gwen, however, was writing a letter. "Don't say a word about it," she said.

Postman Griffith read the address. "Birmingham," he said. "Indeed to goodness no. I hope you haven't said something reckless, girl?"

"Maybe," said Gwen.

But not long afterwards a digging machine came and dug a trench right up the cwm, across the fields. In the trench they put a pipe. At the bottom end, near the house, there was a tap. At the top end a pipe went into the lake.

These things happened on a market day, so that Owen did not see the men from the Birmingham Water Board. Gwen said nothing, except that she could wash the babies now. Owen said nothing at all.

"Everything is perfect," he said. "Why try to understand it as well?"

And the Ark? It is there in Cwmfach. "Mystery how it got there," says Owen, explaining nothing, keeping hay in it and standing his beehives on the deck out of the way of badgers. He is waiting, too, for a plague of baby Afancs coming out of the taps in Birmingham.